BIKER GIRL

BIKER GIRL

story and art by **Misako Rocks!**

HYPERION PAPERBACKS
New York

Printed in the United States of America
First Hyperion Paperbacks edition, 2006
Printed in the United States of America
This book is set in WildWords and Comicrazy.
Retouch and lettering by Chris Dickey

10 9 8 7 6 5 4 3 2 1
Library of Congress Cataloging-in-Publication Data on file.
ISBN 0-7868-3676-8
Visit www.hyperionteens.com

Thanks To...

My Mother, Father, Shin in Japan

My Great Editor, Alessandra

My Super Agent, Steven Malk

My Awesome web Designer, Alicia Kubista

My Comic Monster Pal, Craig Thompson

My Family at THE ONION

My Pals in WI, MO, NY, JAPAN

My Soul Mate, Banban

And... My Kurinko!

BIKER GIRL

TORU!
HEY, KIDS!
WHOOSH!!

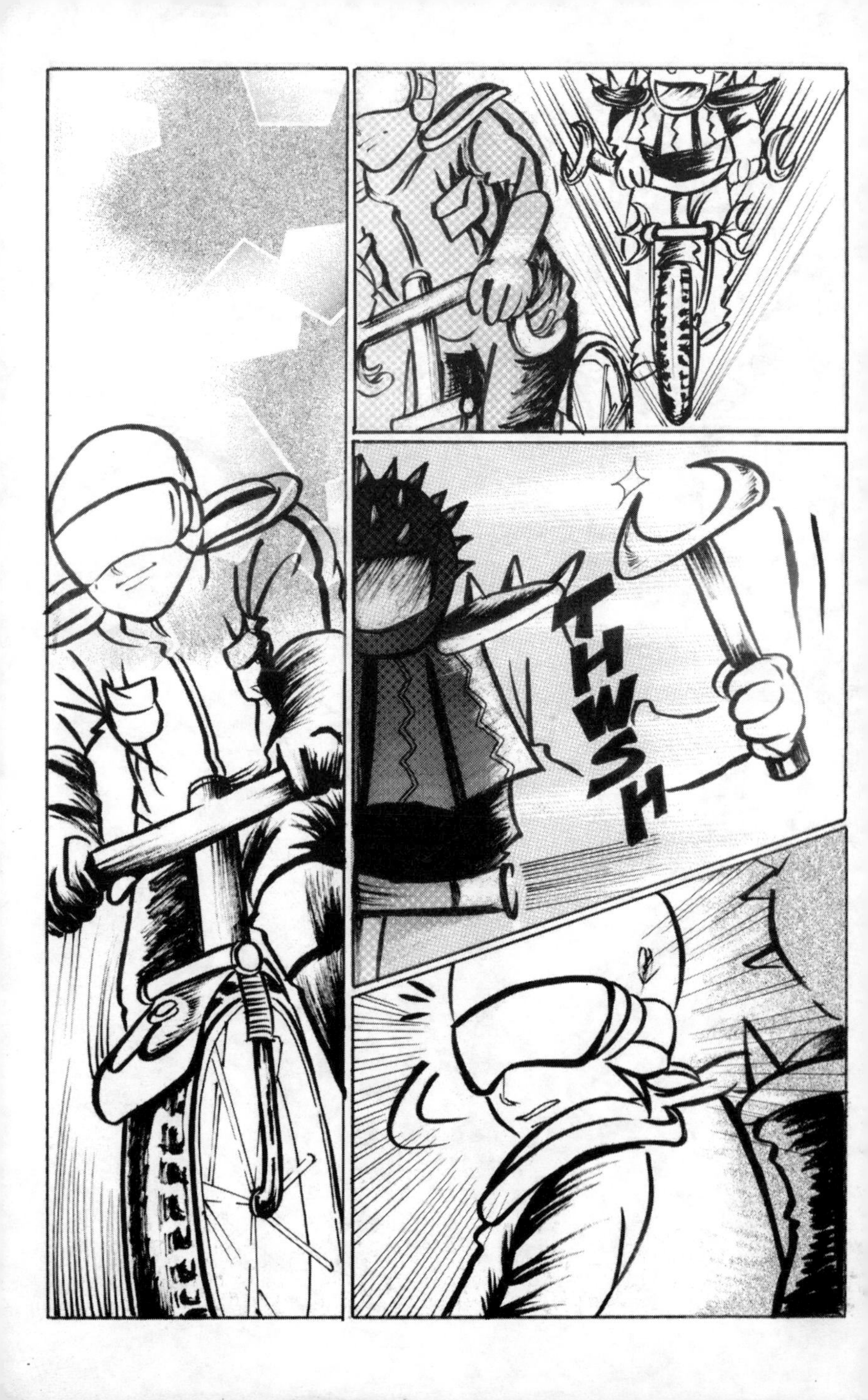
THWSH

HA
What's happening?

NO!!!!

BEEEP!!
AKI!! TIME TO GET UP! PLEASE COME DOWNSTAIRS AND EAT BREAKFAST!
MNN...OK.

AKI. YOU ARE GOING TO HELP GRANDPA CLEAN UP THE GARAGE, RIGHT?? SO YOU BETTER HURRY UP.
IT'S SUNDAY. TAKE IT EASY.
Aki Kuruma, age 17, a high school student. Lives with parents, a big brother, and a grandfather.
HA HA

GOOD MORNING.
HEY—!! YOU'RE LATE!! EVERYBODY FINISHED BREAKFAST ALREADY.
This is my brother, Arata.
HEY, GRANDPA!
OH...

GRANDPA, ARE WE GONNA CLEAN ALL OF THIS UP TODAY?
YEAH!

AKI!
HEY, DID YOU FINISH THE HOMEWORK?
...YEAH, WHY?
CAN YOU SHOW IT TO ME? DON'T YOU WANNA HELP YOUR BEST FRIEND?
NO! KAI, I'M NOT GOING TO DO YOUR WORK FOR YOU EVERY DAY.

NO WAY! YOU ALWAYS SAY THAT. BESIDES, I'M BUSY NOW.
PLEASE... QUEEN AKI! I'LL DO ANYTHING! THIS IS THE LAST TIME—PROMISE!
WHAT ARE YOU DOING?
CLEANING UP GRANDPA'S STUFF IN THE GARAGE!
HEY, I CAN HELP YOU, SO COULD...
NO, DO YOUR HOMEWORK!

GRANDPA!
WHAT'S
THIS?
OH...

OH...
ARE YOU OK?
AKI!
I CAN'T BELIEVE IT!
THIS WAS MY FATHER'S BIKE! A VERY SPECIAL BIKE.
THIS BIKE HELPED SAVE PEOPLE FOR A LONG, LONG TIME. I INHERITED THIS BIKE. BUT VERY FEW PEOPLE CAN RIDE IT.

OH...I'LL NEVER FORGET THAT MOMENT! BIKE GANG AND BIKE HERO. THIS WAS MEANT TO BE. I CAN'T BELIEVE YOU FOUND IT! I'VE ALWAYS WONDERED WHO WOULD BE THE NEXT HERO...AND IT'S *YOU*, AKI!
AH...HMM, GRANDPA I HAVE NO IDEA WHAT YOU ARE TALKING ABOUT. WHAT BIKE GANG?? ANYWAY, WE HAVE TO FINISH CLEANING THE GARAGE, RIGHT?
AKI! YOUR TIME HAS COME! NOW YOU HAVE BEEN CHOSEN. THE BIKE GANG WILL FIND OUT ABOUT YOU AND THEY WILL COME!
THE BIKE GANG IS TERRIBLY DANGEROUS. THEY STEAL AND...
OK, OK, GRANDPA. YOU SHOULD TAKE A BREAK. LET ME CLEAN UP.

I didn't want to admit it, but there was something about that bike...
HEY, GUYS, DID YOU FINISH CLEANING UP?
OOOOPS!

Toru, will you win the race?
YES, LITTLE AKI.

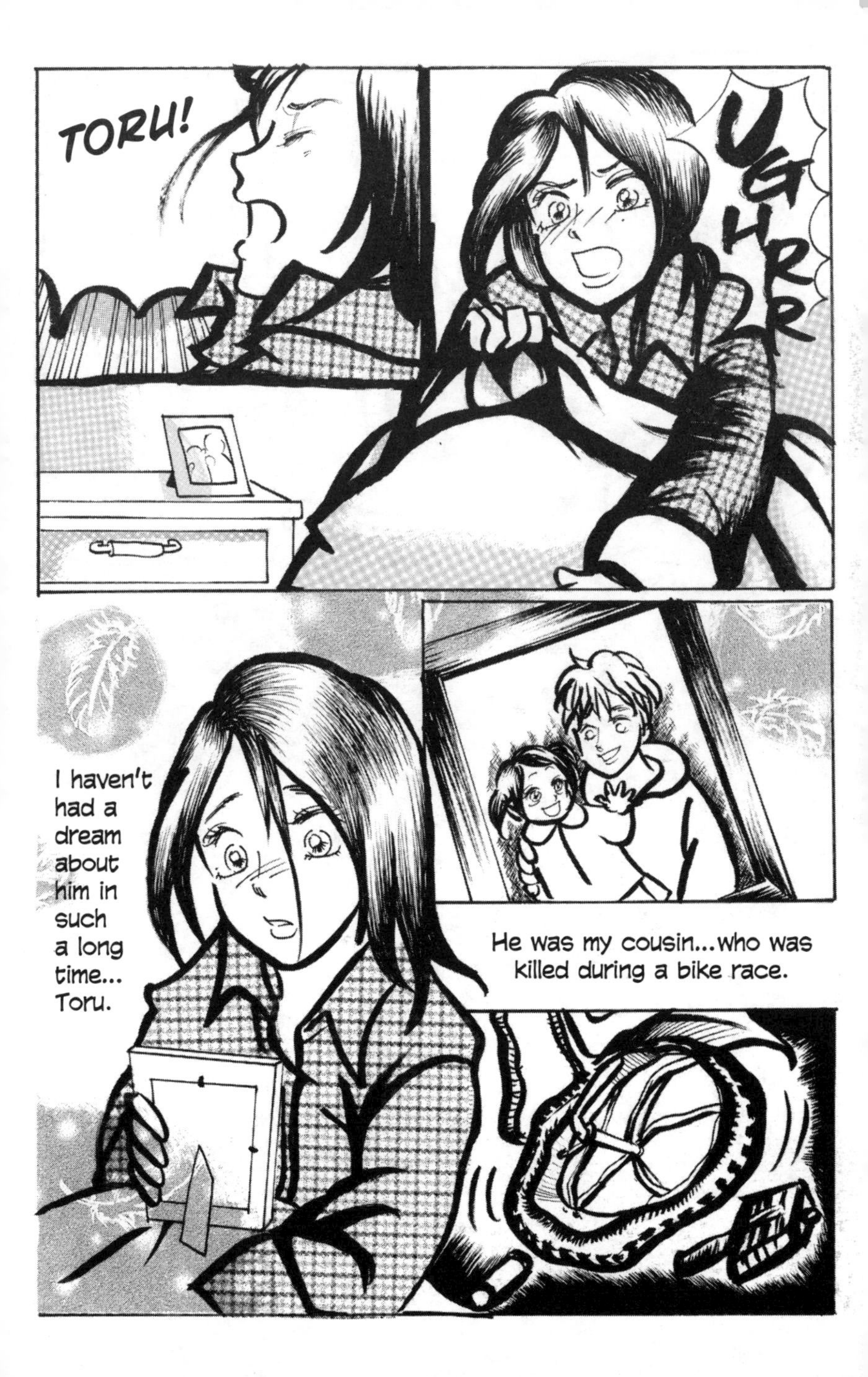
TORU!
UGHRRR
I haven't had a dream about him in such a long time... Toru.
He was my cousin...who was killed during a bike race.

HEY, AKI.
MORNING, NAMI.
DID YOU STUDY FOR THE MATH TEST?
OH NO! I *FORGOT!*
WHAT DID YOU DO LAST NIGHT?
MMM... NOTHING. I JUST COULDN'T SLEEP. I HAD A WEIRD DREAM.

3-A
Mnnnnn...
I can't focus! That crazy bike and the dream about Toru keep bothering me. What's ***wrong*** with me!?
Briiing
Shoot...I didn't even finish.
MATH III NAME

What is it about that bike? I get such a weird feeling whenever I think about it. I have to go back and check it out again.
SEE YOU TOMORROW, NAMI! I GOTTA GO!
OK! CALL ME!
She was so out of it today... Is she OK?
HI, MOM, I'M HOME!
WHERE ARE YOU GOING, AKI?
MY ROOM!

WHY IS SHE IN SUCH A RUSH?
OK! LET'S GO!

If I ignore this feeling, I won't be able to sleep again!
WHAT ARE YOU DOING UP THERE?
AKI! ARE YOU OK?

GRANDPA!
COULD YOU GIVE ME THE KEY TO THE GARAGE?
WHY?
UH, I FORGOT SOMETHING IN THERE...
HERE YOU GO.
OK, I'LL GIVE IT BACK!
HAVE FUN, AKI...

ka-tek
I don't know why,
but I feel like something powerful
is drawing me to this bike.

FWOOOOOSH

WHAT'S HAPPENING?
WHAT'S GOING ON?!

AKI.
GRANDPA, WHAT'S THIS?
I KNEW IT.
I HAVE NO IDEA WHAT HAPPENED. I JUST TOUCHED THE BIKE!
AKI! I NEED TO TELL YOU SOMETHING. SOMETHING IMPORTANT.
WHAT ARE YOU TALKING ABOUT?

A LONG TIME AGO, IN THE EARLY 1900'S, MY FAMILY RAN A BIKE DELIVERY BUSINESS. AT THAT TIME, THERE WERE MANY CRIMES HAPPENING IN MY HOMETOWN.
GIVE ME YOUR MONEY!
Somebody has to stop them. What can I do?
GAK
So my great-grandfather started making a machine to save people from those bad guys. He invented the first superbike!

But the thieves had bikes too. My great-grandfather's bike was not strong enough to fight them.
The bike gang was getting bigger and more powerful. Crime was controlling the city.
My father wanted to make his bike stronger, but he didn't know how...
Dad!
LOOK, DAD! THIS IS MY SOUL MATE, MR. EL!
WE ARE CONNECTED, SO WE CAN UNDERSTAND EACH OTHER WITHOUT WORDS.
SOUL... MATE...

THAT'S IT!

It was his idea that a bike and a biker's soul should be connected.
The union of two spirits is the most important thing.
What is it that bikes don't usually have? Wings, motor, anything alive...

He added those things, but the key is "united spirits."
He called it the "SPIRIT BIKE." That's why so few people can ride it.

TORU WAS ALREADY A BIKER, BUT HE WAS ALSO THE BRAVEST PERSON IN OUR FAMILY, SO HE COULD OPERATE THE BIKE. LATER I INHERITED IT. TORU WAS THE LAST BIKE HERO.

WHAT? MY COUSIN TORU? WHAT DID HE DO?
TORU ENTERED A BIKE COMPETITION WITH A MEMBER OF THE BIKE GANG. THEY KNEW HE WAS A BETTER BIKER, SO ONE OF THE GANG PUSHED HIM OFF A HILL AND HE DIED.
WHAT?! I THOUGHT HIS DEATH WAS AN ACCIDENT! DO YOU MEAN SOMEONE FROM THE GANG KILLED HIM!? I CAN'T BELIEVE IT!
WAIT, GRANDPA, DOES THAT MEAN THE BIKE GANG IS STILL AROUND? AND IF SO, THEY'LL COME BACK, RIGHT?
I ALWAYS WONDERED WHO WOULD BE THE NEXT HERO! AND IT'S YOU!
AKI. IT'S TIME FOR YOU TO REALIZE YOUR DESTINY. ONCE THE BIKE CHANGES, A RADIO SIGNAL IS RELEASED AND THE BIKE GANG WILL BE ABLE TO FIND YOU.
JUST TAKE OFF YOUR HELMET WHEN YOU WANT TO GO BACK TO BEING YOURSELF.
BUT I CAN'T DO THIS! I'M NOT BRAVE. BESIDES, I CAN HARDLY RIDE A BIKE... WAIT!

I HAVE NO IDEA
WHAT'S HAPPENING TO ME...
I HOPE THIS IS JUST A
DREAM.
I feel like every part of my
body is being pulled by
something. Hey, what is this?

I'm back to being Aki...
That night I couldn't sleep at all. I still can't believe that Toru died because of the bike gang... and I'm supposed to be the next bike hero? *I'm just a high school girl!*
WHAT IS THE BIKE GANG?
AKI, DO YOU WANT TO EAT SOMETHING?
NO, THANKS.
AKI IS ACTING SO FUNNY. I'M WORRIED.
REALLY?

UGH, I DON'T WANT TO GO TO SCHOOL TODAY.
SEE YOU LATER, GRANDPA!
HMMM...
AKI, WAIT!
LISTEN. THE JEWELRY STORE AT THAT CORNER WAS ROBBED BY SOME GUYS. SO DON'T USE THAT STREET, OK?
AKI, IT'S TIME.
NO, GRANDPA.

I'M NOT A SUPERHERO! I'M JUST A NORMAL GIRL!
WHY ME?!
AKI! YOU HAVE TO BE STRONG! HAVE FAITH THAT YOU WILL KNOW WHAT TO DO.
SINCE TORU DIED, I'VE BEEN WAITING FOR THIS MOMENT. YOU AND THE BIKE FOUND EACH OTHER! THIS IS MEANT TO BE! YOU MUST FEEL IT.
I TOLD YOU! I DON'T KNOW WHAT YOU'RE TALKING ABOUT!
AKI. YOU AND TORU WERE VERY CLOSE. YOU HAVE HIS SPIRIT INSIDE YOU.
WHAT?
TORU'S SPIRIT?
I don't know why I'm back here. But it's true that I feel a connection with this bike and have to find out who killed Toru.

I was so scared to touch the bike again... but I did.
FLASH
BREEEEE!
FUSION

When I opened my eyes,
I was on the bike.
What am I doing?
I feel like my body
instinctively knows how
to handle this bike.

AKI!
GRANDPA. YOU'RE RIGHT. I THINK I AM CONNECTED TO THIS BIKE. IT'S SO STRANGE.
JUST LISTEN TO THAT FEELING. THE BIKE WILL TELL YOU WHAT TO DO.
MMMM...

WHOA! AM I FLYING?!
FWOOOOOO

WHAT WAS THAT?
I DON'T KNOW.
AGHH!

Miyata
STOP! YOU ARE SURROUNDED BY POLICE, THERE IS NO WAY...
AGHHH

DIAMOND
GET OUT OF THE WAY!!
WHAT?

BOOOOO... M
WHAT THE HELL!?

HI... EXCUSE ME.
WHO ARE YOU? YOU MUST BE PART OF THAT BIKE GANG!
NO...I'M... I'M A...
HEY, WAIT!
ARGHHH!!
YOU CAN'T GO INSIDE!
What am I *doing* here?

HELP!
HEY, ARE YOU OK? CAN YOU STAND UP?
I'M OK, BUT THAT GANG DESTROYED MY STORE!
Oh
no!

I almost passed out
when I saw the gang.

HEH HEH

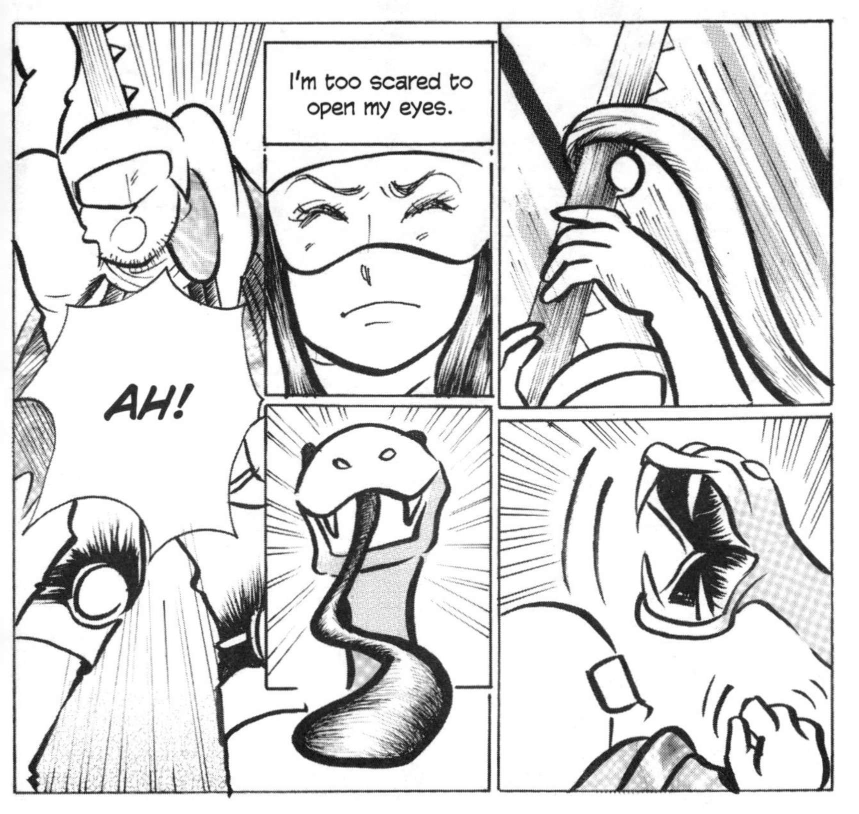
I'm too scared to open my eyes.
AH!

WHAT DID
THE SNAKE DO?
IS THIS REAL?
WHAT IS THIS
BIKE CAPABLE OF?
ARGHH

AGH-HH..
When I opened my eyes,
all the guys had been knocked out.

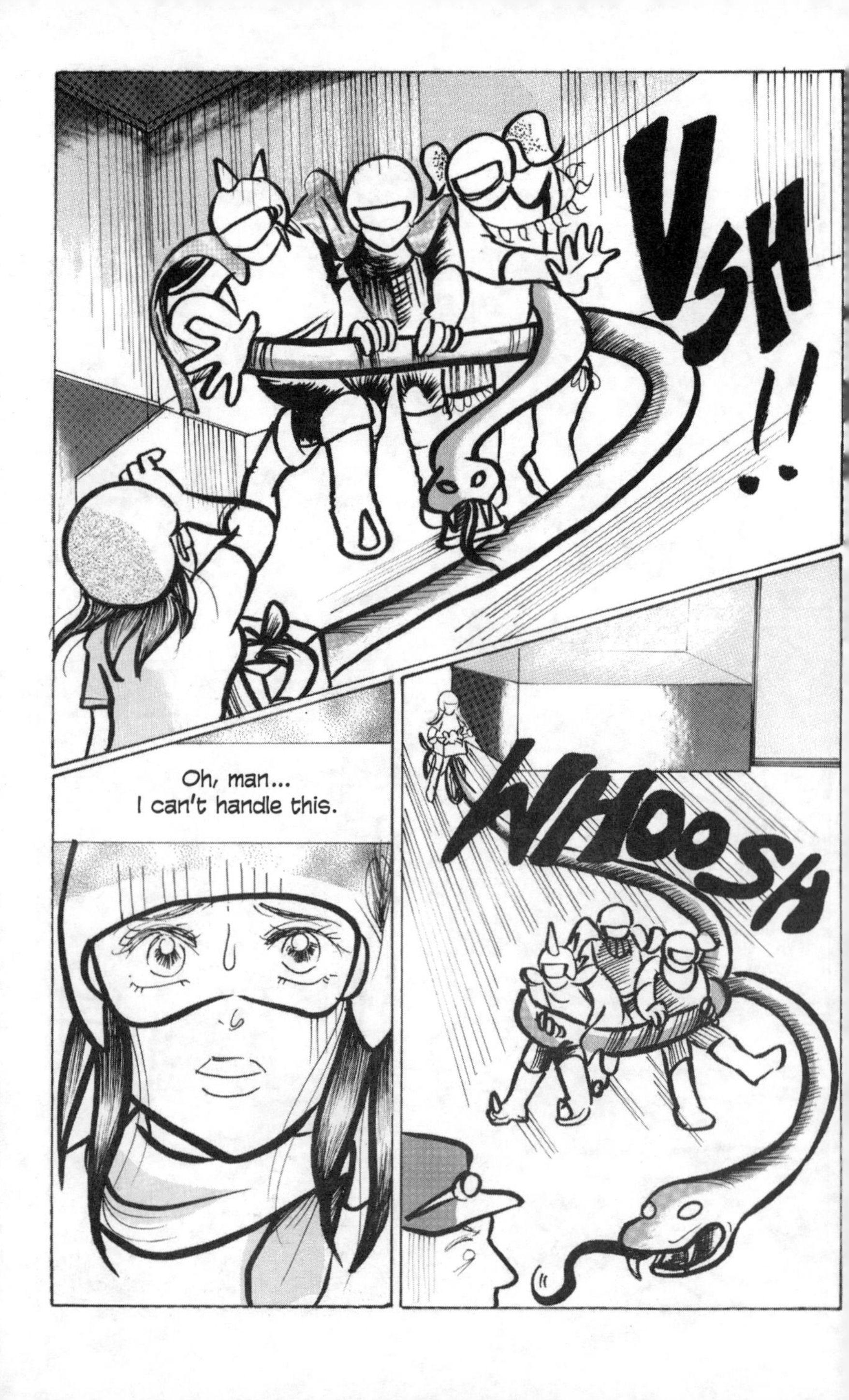
VSH!!
WHOOSH
Oh, man...
I can't handle this.

HEY! WAIT!
WHO ARE YOU?
I... I HAVE
TO GO NOW.
BYE!
Whoa!

AKI.
YOU'RE BACK.
ARE YOU ALL
RIGHT?

IS SOMEBODY THERE??
MEOW!
DID SOMEONE SEE US?
NO, IT'S JUST A CAT. DON'T WORRY.
Who is that girl? Is that *Aki*?
Suddenly I felt exhausted. What had I done?
sigh

It's morning, and it's still hard for me to believe what happened.
AKI.
KNOCK KNOCK
COME IN.
TELL ME WHAT TO DO, TORU.
ARE YOU OK?
GRANDPA...

YOU DID A GREAT JOB TODAY. DID YOU KNOW THAT? YOU SAVED THAT STORE AND THOSE PEOPLE.
GRANDPA, TELL ME MORE ABOUT THE MAGIC BIKE. I NEED TO KNOW HOW IT WORKS.
AKI, YOU NEED TO TRUST THAT BIKE. OTHERWISE YOU WON'T BE ABLE TO CONTROL IT.
TORU DID HIS BEST, AND NOW IT IS YOUR TURN.
I DON'T KNOW...I'M NOT GOOD AT THIS. TORU WAS A REAL HERO...NOT ME.

HEY, YOUR BOYFRIEND IS HERE!
ARATA, SHUT UP! HE'S NOT MY BOYFRIEND!
YO!
YO! GRANDPA KENZO.
YO!
KAI, WHAT DO YOU WANT? I'M NOT GIVING YOU MY HOMEWORK.
THIS MORNING I SAW SOME CRAZY-LOOKING GIRL IN YOUR BACKYARD!
KAI, YOU ARE LIKE A GRANDSON TO ME AND YOU LOVED TORU AS MUCH AS AKI DID. I'LL TELL YOU WHAT YOU SAW.

Grandpa started telling him about that bike and Toru.
What is he going to think?
CIAO!
ALL RIGHT, I'M BETTING YOU GUYS WANT TO BE ALONE NOW, SO I WILL LEAVE.
WHAT!?
I WON'T TELL ANYBODY, I PROMISE.

IF YOU NEED HELP, JUST LET ME KNOW, OK?
UH, OK.

When we were kids, Kai used to chase me around and make me cry.
I used to run to Toru. 'Cause he was always my knight. Kai was my playmate for a long time.
But I feel weird around Kai now. Everything feels different.

A BIKE GANG BROKE INTO THE GYM!
When I heard that, I started running.

They were back. Were they looking for me?

WHO DID THIS? DID THEY BREAK THE WINDOWS?
YAHOO!

I was finally able to get a good look at one guy...
Was he the leader?
He looked familiar...
AKI!
ARE YOU OK?

ARE YOU HURT? CAN YOU MOVE?
I'M OK, JUST HAVE SOME CUTS. BUT WHY DID YOU BRING THE BIKE?
'CAUSE I THOUGHT YOU NEEDED IT!
BUT I... I'M...
AKI! LOOK AT THEM! THEY NEEDED YOUR HELP! YOU KNOW WHAT YOU HAVE TO DO.

YOU'RE RIGHT. I CAN'T IGNORE THIS ANYMORE, KAI.
ALL RIGHT, AKI! I'LL GO CHECK ON THE OTHER KIDS.
BR
EEE!

HEY, YOU!
LET ME GO—AAAH!
ROAA

KAI!
BEHIND
YOU!

WATCH OUT!
HEE-YA!

AGHH

I realized that the leader was staring at me.
It was like he *knew* me...

THAT'S ENOUGH FOR TODAY. LET'S GO.
HEY, BIKER GIRL.
SEE YOU NEXT TIME.

Who was that guy?
I get the strangest feeling about him.
WHAT'S UP, AKI?
I'LL TELL YOU LATER, OK?
YEAH.

WHO IS THAT GIRL?
IS THAT BIKE *FLYING?*
I hope she's OK.
KAI, I HAVE SOMETHING TO TELL YOU.

I FELT SOME KIND OF STRANGE CONNECTION TO THE BIKE LEADER... IT'S LIKE I KNOW HIM.
WHAT? WHO? HOW DID YOU KNOW?
HIS VOICE! I FEEL LIKE I'VE HEARD IT SOMEWHERE... BUT I DON'T KNOW WHERE AND WHEN!
AKI. JUST RELAX. WE CAN TALK ABOUT THAT WHEN WE GET HOME. DON'T WORRY, OK?
LET'S GO HOME.

Kai, why
are you acting so
different?

AKI, THE ANNIVERSARY OF TORU'S DEATH IS COMING SOON.
I KNOW...
TORU WAS MY HERO WHEN I WAS LITTLE—BUT ACTUALLY, HE WAS EVERYBODY'S HERO. AND NOW YOU'RE SOME SUPERGIRL...
I AM NOT!

HEY, IT'S NAMI!
KAI...
WHAT IS IT?
...
NOTHING...
GRIN
OK, LETS GO.
NOW YOU'RE GETTING ALL
SHY ON ME!

Again!
GUYS! COME ON! HURRY UP!
WHAT...?
HEELLLP!
NAMI!

AKI!
NAMI! NAMI!
CALM DOWN! WE HAVE TO GO GET THE MAGIC BIKE! WE CAN'T DO ANYTHING YET, OK?
OK. LET'S GO!

GOOD LUCK!
Take me to the bike gang! I have to rescue Nami!
BEEP

NAMI'S HERE...
HEY!
I'M HERE!!
I KNOW IT'S ME
YOU WANT. PLEASE,
LET HER GO!

HELP! BIKER GIRL!
ALL RIGHT, BIKER GIRL—YOU WANT TO HELP YOUR FRIEND? THE BIGGEST BIKE RACE OF THE YEAR IS COMING UP. YOU'RE GOING TO ENTER IT. IF YOU LOSE, YOU HAVE TO GIVE UP THE MAGIC BIKE. IF YOU WIN, WE WILL LEAVE TOWN AND NEVER RETURN.
ALL RIGHT, I'LL DO IT! AND I'LL WIN THE RACE!

HERE YOU GO!
SEE YOU THERE, BIKER GIRL. LET'S GO, EVERYBODY.
I can't believe I got myself into this *bike race!* But I have no choice now.

THANK YOU, BIKER GIRL!
YOU'RE WELCOME. BYE!

WHAT IS THIS?!
BiKers
WHERE IS THE MYSTERY BIKER?
GRANDPA, I CAN'T BE SCARED ANYMORE... SOMEBODY HAS TO STOP THEM.

GRANDPA, SATURDAY IS THE ANNIVERSARY OF TORU'S DEATH. IT'S THE SAME DAY AS THE BIG BIKE RACE...AND I TOLD THE BIKE GANG THAT I WOULD BE IN IT. IF I WIN, THEY WILL HAVE TO LEAVE TOWN. THIS IS MY CHANCE. I KNOW IT'S THE RIGHT THING TO DO.
AKI, LISTEN. DON'T DO THIS JUST FOR TORU, DO IT FOR YOURSELF AND EVERYONE WHO HAS BEEN HURT BY THE BIKE GANG.

I'M SO PROUD OF YOU. JUST REMEMBER TO BE CAREFUL. YOU'RE IN GRAVE DANGER.
I KNOW, GRANDPA.
HEY, KAI, I HAVE TO TELL YOU SOMETHING...
YEAH?

I TOLD THE LEADER OF THE BIKE GANG THAT I WOULD ENTER THE BIKE RACE THIS WEEKEND.
WHAT? ARE YOU CRAZY?!
I KNOW, KAI, BUT SATURDAY IS TORU'S MEMORIAL DAY, TOO. I THINK THIS IS MY DESTINY. SOMEONE HAS TO STOP THE BIKE GANG.
DO YOU REALIZE HOW DANGEROUS THAT WOULD BE?
I DON'T THINK YOU SHOULD DO IT!
I HAVE NO CHOICE, KAI. PLEASE UNDERSTAND.

ALL RIGHT, BUT, AKI... PLEASE PROMISE ME THAT YOU WILL BE CAREFUL. I WILL DO WHATEVER I CAN.

BYE, AKI.

This is the second time he held my hand...

WE GOTTA GO NOW. *HELLO, AKI?*

HEY, WERE YOU GUYS KISSING OR SOMETHING?
SHUT UP!

OK, *LISTEN UP.* THIS SATURDAY IS A BIG DAY FOR US. IT WILL BE THE DAY WE FINALLY GET RID OF BIKER GIRL.

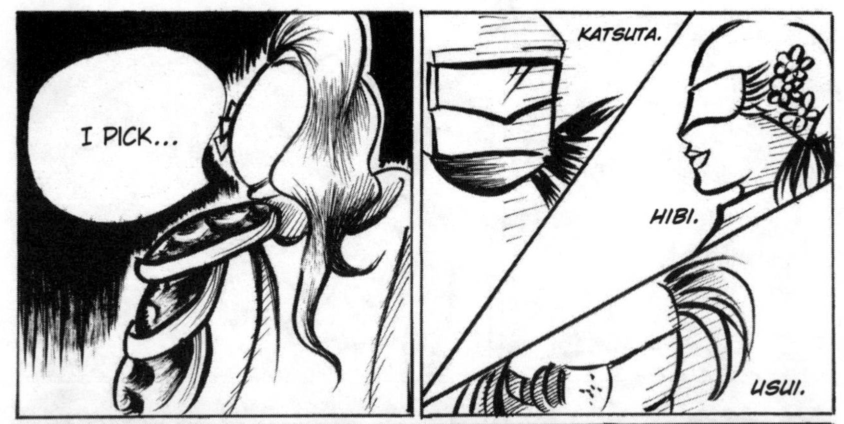
I PICK...
KATSUTA.
HIBI.
USUI.

WE MUST WIN!

A-1
GUYS, I HAVE TO GO...
WE WILL BE AT THE STARTING LINE.
JUST DO YOUR BEST, AKI.
SEE YOU AFTER THE RACE.

AKI!

Kai...
WISH ME LUCK, OK?

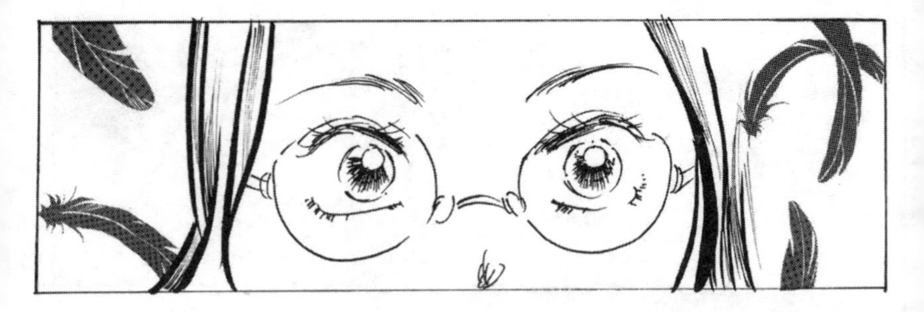

Toru...today I will find the one
who brought you to your death.

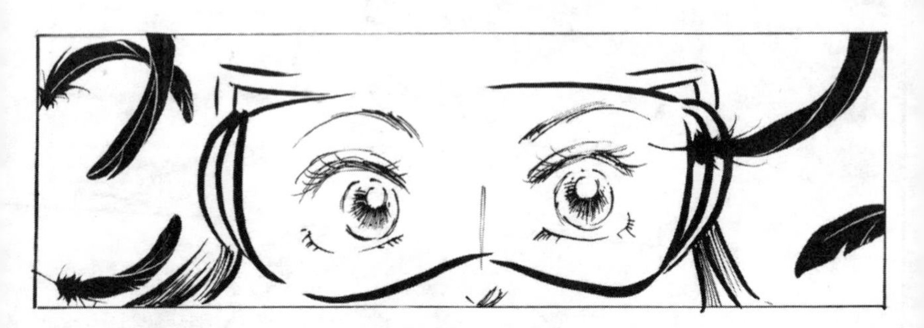

Please help me.

HELLO, EVERYBODY! THE RACE IS ABOUT TO START! SO LET'S CHECK THE BIKE COURSE. WHO IS THIS MYSTERIOUS NEW BIKER GIRL THAT EVERYONE IS TALKING ABOUT?
STA

AND THEY'RE OFF!

Who will make the first move?
HA!
It's the bike gang leader!
He's pretty big,
but he doesn't have my bike!

IT'S BIKER GIRL VERSUS KATSUTA! WHAT WILL HAPPEN NEXT?
DID YOU SEE HER MOVE? AMAZING! SHE ALMOST FLEW!
OWW!!
He's attacking the other bikers! I've got to stop him.

IT'S OVER, BIKER GIRL!
KATSUTA AGAIN! HE'S CLOSING IN ON BIKER GIRL!
WILL SHE GET AWAY FROM HIM?!
NO WAY, KATSUTA!!

HOLY COW!
SHE FLEW
OVER KATSUTA!
SHE'S A BIRD!!
SHHHOOO
Aki!
You are
amazing!
I can't
believe
how strong
you are.

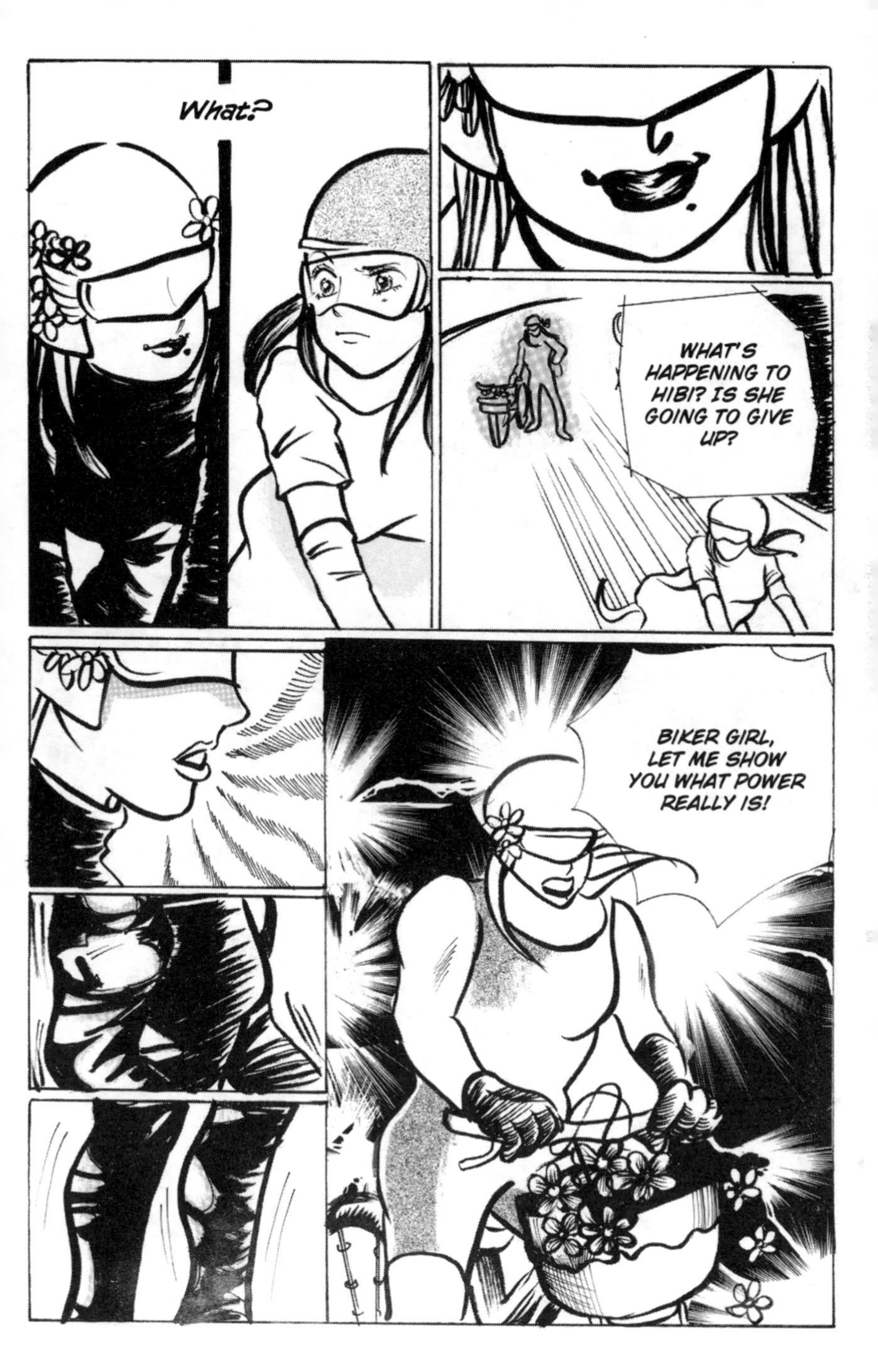
What?
WHAT'S HAPPENING TO HIBI? IS SHE GOING TO GIVE UP?
BIKER GIRL, LET ME SHOW YOU WHAT POWER REALLY IS!

OH MY GOD! WHAT'S HAPPENING TO HER? SHE'S GETTING BIGGER, AND HER MUSCLES ARE RIPPING THROUGH HER CLOTHES!
WHAT'S GOING ON?! WATCH OUT, BIKER GIRL!
OH, NO! SHE'S CATCHING UP!
GAH!

Huf
Huf
HA-HA!
YOU'RE LOOKING SCRAWNY, BIKER GIRL!

LET GO OF ME!
AGHHH!
HIBI IS STILL IN THE RACE! SHE'S CATCHING UP TO BIKER GIRL!
KRASH

AKI!
BIKER GIRL IS DOWN!
SHE FELL OFF THE BRIDGE!
IS HIBI THE WINNER?

UNBELIEVABLE! WHAT IS BIKER GIRL DOING?

Hyuuu

YOU CAN'T CATCH ME!
NOOO!

SPLOOSH

SHE DID IT!
BIKER GIRL IS BACK...
AND HIBI IS DOWN!

NOW THERE ARE ONLY THREE BIKERS LEFT IN THE RACE!
HOW DO YOU LIKE THIS, BIKER GIRL?

AAHH
WHAT IS THIS?!
I'M TRAPPED!
Smile....
BYE! HAVE FUN!

OH MY GOSH...
THE BIKE IS CUTTING
A HOLE IN THE NET!
IT'S UNBEATABLE!
GO,
BIKER GIRL!

I HAVE A PRESENT FOR YOU, USUI!
WHAT?
ARGHHH!!
NO, I'M TRAPPED...
WHERE IS THE REMOTE?

LOOKING FOR THIS?
WHAT?!
HOW DID YOU GET THAT?
hee
hee
SORRY... MY SNAKE HAS NO MANNERS.
GIVE IT BACK... NOW!
NOPE!
TIME TO GO HOME, USUI!

YES, SHE IS.
KENZO, SHE IS AMAZING!
YEAH!!!

It's him.

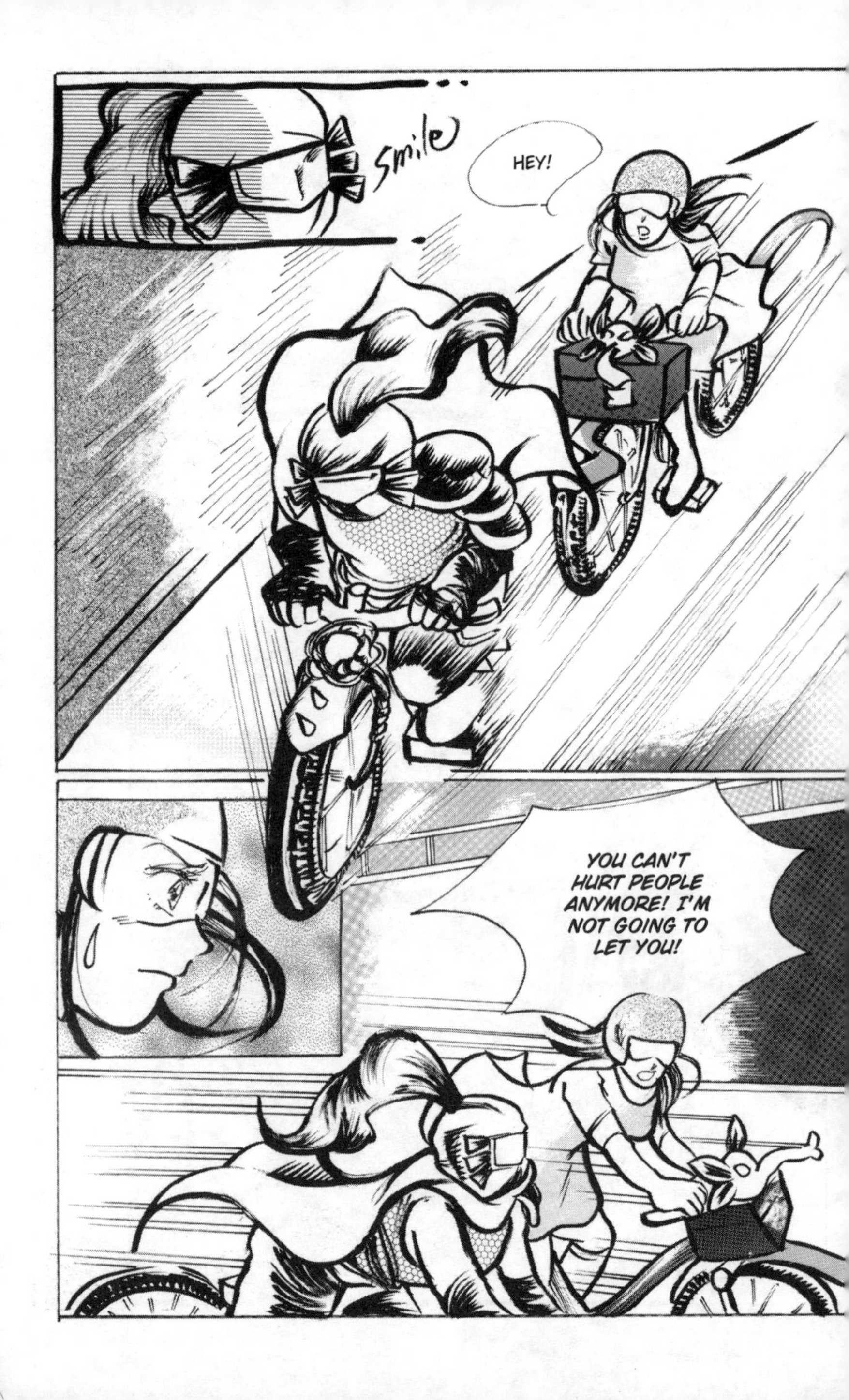
Smile
HEY!
YOU CAN'T HURT PEOPLE ANYMORE! I'M NOT GOING TO LET YOU!

WAIT!
Do I know you?
HEY! WHERE DID HE GO?

WHAT'S HAPPENING TO BIKER GIRL?
WHAT'S GOING ON?
AKI, DO YOU REALLY THINK YOU CAN BEAT ME?

ARATA!
AKI!!!

I...
I CAN'T DO THIS!
WHAT'S HAPPENING?
SHE JUST FOUND OUT WHO HE IS...
WHAT? WHO? DO YOU KNOW HIM?
I'M AFRAID I DO, KAI.

HAS BIKER GIRL GIVEN UP? SOMEONE IS RUNNING ONTO THE COURSE!
AKI! WHAT HAPPENED? ARE YOU OK?
ARA...
THE BIKE GANG LEADER— IT'S ARATA!

MY OWN BROTHER. I CAN'T DO THIS ANYMORE.
ARATA! ARATA!
KAI! STOP!
HEY!

AGHH!!

KAI!
Even though Arata is my brother...
I have to do something.
How did he become this monster?

I don't need a helmet anymore...
ARATA! STOP! HOW COULD YOU? YOU KILLED TORU!
ARATA! IT'S ME, AKI!

LOOK AT THAT SPEED!
I have to face him as Aki! But I am still Biker Girl, and Toru is inside of me.

BOTH RIDERS HAVE REACHED THE RAMP! WHICH ONE WILL JUMP FIRST!?
BYE, AKI!
AHH!!
AND BIKER GIRL IS DOWN!

THIS RACE IS MINE!
NOT YET!

!!
WHOOOSH

I SAID, NOT YET, ARATA!
WHAT?

NO!
ARATA!
LET GO OF YOUR
BIKE!!

NO!!!
THE SUPERHERO WAS JUST A KID! CAN YOU BELIEVE IT?
AND THE WINNER IS BIKER GIRL!

UGH...

WHERE AM I?
YOU'RE IN THE HOSPITAL. YOU'VE BEEN SLEEPING FOR THREE DAYS.
WHAT HAPPENED?
THE BIKE RACE. YOU FELL OFF THE RAMP, REMEMBER? WHY DIDN'T YOU LET GO OF YOUR BIKE?
THAT BIKE BELONGED TO TORU. AFTER HE DIED, I TOOK IT... I THOUGHT I COULD SOMEHOW BECOME TORU. BUT INSTEAD I ENDED UP BECOMING THE LEADER OF THE BIKE GANG AND...

WHY DID
YOU JOIN THE
BIKE GANG?
SINCE WE WERE LITTLE,
I WAS ALWAYS BEING COMPARED TO TORU.
HE WAS BETTER THAN ME AT EVERYTHING.
EVERYONE EVEN LIKED HIM BETTER!
WHEN I WAS SEVENTEEN, I MET
SOME MEMBERS OF THE BIKE GANG.

THE LEADER OF THE BIKE GANG KNEW THAT I WAS JEALOUS OF TORU'S SKILLS, SO HE TRAINED ME. THANKS TO HIM, I BECAME A GREAT BIKER.
I WANTED TO BEAT TORU AND SHOW HIM I COULD BE BETTER AT SOMETHING...BUT THEN ONE OF THE BIKE GANG KNOCKED HIM DOWN DURING THE BIKE RACE, AND TORU DIED...
I COULDN'T HELP TORU, AND I WAS SO SCARED...BECAUSE SOMEHOW I KNEW IT WAS MY FAULT. SO I STAYED IN THE BIKE GANG AND BECAME THE LEADER, BECAUSE I FELT LIKE I BELONGED THERE. THEN MY OWN LITTLE SISTER FINALLY BEAT ME. EVERYTHING IS OVER NOW...

WHY!? WHY DID YOU DO THAT? HOW COULD YOU HAVE BEEN THEIR LEADER? HOW??
AKI, I GOT STUCK IN THE PAST FOR A LONG TIME...I HATED MYSELF FOR WHAT HAPPENED. I DIDN'T KNOW WHAT TO DO AFTER TORU DIED. MAYBE I WAS WAITING FOR SOMEONE WHO COULD STOP ME. SOMEONE LIKE YOU.
THEN SEEING YOU AND HOW BRAVE YOU WERE MADE ME REALIZE I WAS WRONG.

ARATA, EVEN THOUGH YOU WERE THE LEADER OF THE BIKE GANG, I CAN'T HATE YOU...I WAS TOO SCARED TO LOSE YOU. YOU ARE MY OWN BROTHER. BUT EVERYTHING CAN'T BE LIKE IT WAS... I NEED TIME.
I KNOW...
YOU NEED TO REST. LET'S TALK LATER.

I DON'T KNOW WHAT TO SAY. I HAVE NEVER HAD TO FACE SOMETHING LIKE THIS BEFORE. I AM PROUD OF YOU. AKI...DO YOU BELIEVE HIM?
YES...I DO.
YO!

ARE YOU OK? I CAN'T BELIEVE YOU'RE NOT HURT.

I'M TOUGH— MAYBE I'LL BE THE NEXT BIKER GIRL.

KAI, WHEN YOU PASSED OUT, I WAS SO SCARED. I REALIZED HOW IMPORTANT YOU ARE TO ME.

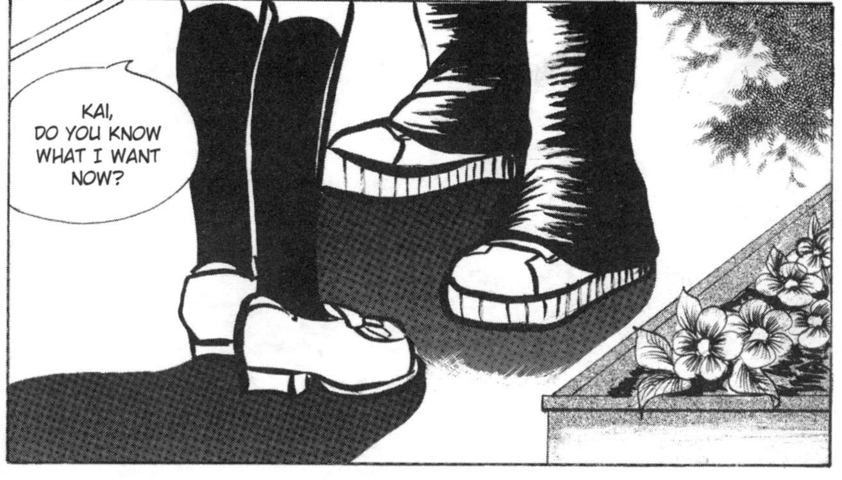
KAI, DO YOU KNOW WHAT I WANT NOW?

THIS?
Have you heard of Biker Girl?
If you need her, she'll find you.

Coming soon from ***MISAKO ROCKS!***